5
5/18

The Littlest
DINOSAUR

To Chloe
with love

First published in Great Britain in 2008 by Bloomsbury Publishing Plc.
Published in the U.S.A. in 2008 by Walker Publishing Company, Inc.
Distributed to the trade by Macmillan

For information about permission to reproduce selections from this book, write to
Permissions, Walker & Company, 175 Fifth Avenue, New York, New York 10010

ISBN-13: 978-0-8027-9759-9

Typeset in Goudy Old Style
Art created with watercolor and ink

Printed in Mexico

The Littlest
DiNOSAUR

MiCHAEL FOREMAN

Walker & Company • New York

Long, long ago when the world was young and everything was new, a mother dinosaur sat proudly on her eggs.

One by one, the eggs began to crack, and baby dinosaurs poked their heads out into the sunshine. All except one.

The mother worried and fussed about it and kept it warm and sang songs to it. But still the egg didn't crack.

The neighbors came by with help and advice.

"Make it warmer," they said.

"Keep it cool," they suggested.

The mother was very loving and lay beside the egg all the time. She breathed on it to keep it warm or fanned it with banana leaves to cool it down. But still the egg didn't crack.

The father dinosaur wanted to break the egg open,
but the mother said, "No. It will happen when the baby
is ready, not before."

One day, the father became so tired of looking after
all the other young dinosaurs while the mother
fussed over the egg that he put his face very
close to the egg and shouted, "Come on, egg!
Do something!"

The egg shook. The egg wobbled, and then
it began to crack. A little crack at first,
then a big crack, and the shell broke in two.
The baby dinosaur blinked in the sunlight.

The father dinosaur gasped. The mother dinosaur gasped.
All the young dinosaurs and all the neighbors gasped.
They had never seen such a tiny baby.

"That's the littlest dinosaur I have ever seen," said the father.
"He's no bigger than a dinosaur's toe!"

The neighbors began to giggle.

"Oh! He may be tiny, but he's very special to me," cried the mother dinosaur, and she scooped up the baby and kissed his tiny face.

Days and weeks passed, and no matter how much food the mother dinosaur gave the baby, he didn't grow any bigger.

The littlest dinosaur was sad because he
was too small to join his big brothers
and sisters when they played.
And what if one of his huge
neighbors stepped on him
by accident?

The only place the littlest
dinosaur felt safe was high
on a hill. There he could sit
and look down on the forest.
It made him feel bigger.

One day, far away on another hill, he saw another dinosaur. It was a Long Neck. Even at that distance, he looked sad. The littlest dinosaur wondered how a dinosaur that big could possibly be sad.

When the rainy season began, the big dinosaurs squelched and rolled in the mud. But not the littlest dinosaur. He hated the mud. He was always getting stuck in the other dinosaurs' big, muddy footprints and having to yell, "Help! Get me out of here!"

One day, the father dinosaur got stuck. He was squelching and rolling in the deep mud at the edge of the river. But when he tried to get out, he couldn't. The more he struggled, the more he got stuck.

"Get me out of here!" he yelled.

The mother tried to help, but **she** got stuck. The neighbors tried to help, and **they** got stuck. The littlest dinosaur's brothers and sisters waded in and **they** got stuck too.

"Get us out of here!" they all yelled.

The littlest dinosaur wished and wished that he were big enough to rescue them.

"You have to go for help," said the mother dinosaur.
But who could help? wondered the littlest dinosaur.
Then he remembered the Long Neck.

The littlest dinosaur was scared as he stepped from the riverbank onto a water lily leaf. It tipped and dipped, but it didn't sink.

One leaf at a time, he wibbled and wobbled his way across the river, then ran through the forest and climbed the hill, slipping and sliding, sliding and slipping, until he got to the top.

There he was—the Long Neck. He looked down at the littlest dinosaur.

"Help me, please," the littlest dinosaur cried. "My family is stuck in the river and the water is rising fast!"

The Long Neck picked him up and, with great, long strides, was soon down the hill, through the forest, and at the riverbank. He stretched his neck across the river and began pulling out the sinking dinosaurs, until one by one they were all safe on the shore.

"Thank you!" the father dinosaur shouted as he waved to the Long Neck. "And as for you," he said, picking up the littlest dinosaur, "you may be the size of a bug, but you're as brave as a dinosaur one hundred times your size." And he kissed him on his tiny nose.

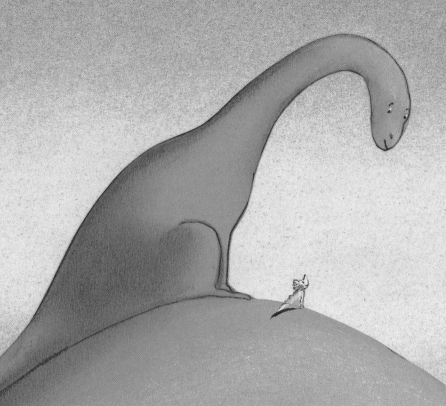

When the rains stopped and
the river was not so wide, the littlest
dinosaur went to visit the Long Neck again.
He no longer looked so sad.
"I thought I was too big and clumsy to do anything
useful," he said, "but now I know that's not true."
"And I thought I was too small to do anything at all,"
laughed the littlest dinosaur.
They sat together on the hill, the biggest and the littlest,
and now the greatest of friends.